Shattered Windows

Flash Fiction

by

Deborah L. Fruchey

ISBN: 979-8-9875209-6-3
Library of Congress Control Number: : 2023922508

Cover Image: MysticArtDesign on Pixabay.com

Author's Note:
Do not assume that stories told
using the first person are
personal anecdotes.
Do not assume that third person stories
are not.

www.lastlaughproductions.org
logo by Bradleigh Stockwell

Many, many thanks to the following people:

Jan Steckel, for afternoons of writing and hospitality

Steve Arntson and Richard Loranger, for writerly companionship & inspiration & a ready ear

David Carillo, Linda Folk, Marty Malin, Gregory Montoya, Aletheia Morden, Nicky Ruxton and Jim White, for friendship, encouragement beyond compare, sharing ideas and resources, and numberless wonderful afternoons of conversation

Maria & Evelyn & Monica, still writing together after all these years, marvelously intimate without encroachment

love you all

Acknowledgements

The story "Bag Lunch" was first published in **Homage to M&Ms***, a chapbook by Word Garden East, 2009*

Table of Contents

Snoring

They were all packed into the back of their RV that summer. It was a year of California drought, 1977, and they had left home to tour the country. At home, people were rationing water, letting their lawns die so they could keep showering, spray-painting the dead grass green so it wasn't so depressing. But it still crunched when you walked on it. Somewhere it must be better: moister, more amusing. Somewhere out there must be a place where they'd like each other better.

But getting there was hell, with five children and two adults in one rolling room. The littlest girl fit into a cupboard, the parents in a loft over the cab. At bedtime the banquette in the back folded down, and four children who had sworn eternal hostility got to sleep packed together like batteries.

The middle brother snored.

He was a very dedicated snoresman. He never took a break. He was not perturbed, wakened, or even liable to change notes, no matter how they pummeled and turned him. This left three children wide awake.

The 13 year old planned her suicide and fantasized funerals in the rain, and how everyone would suffer despair and remorse.

The 15 year old squirmed and tried not to touch anyone with her breasts.

Her nightgown was cotton and printed with fatuous pink flowers. God, if anyone from school ever saw it! *Ruffles!* she thought with loathing. I mean really, she was 15 after all, hadn't mom ever heard of Victoria's Secret? She sank into grumpy dreams of a reupholstered closet.

The oldest girl was 18, and what was she doing here? She asked herself, day after sultry day. She was legally old enough to leave. She had — maybe — enough money for a Greyhound bus. She could sneak off while they were staring at the Grand Canyon and go buy some dignity.

But where would she go? The house was rented out for the summer. Her friends were all on vacation. And worse, what about afterwards, when they came back and told her what they thought of her? How she didn't have a shred of love or kindness or family feeling or decent religion in her body. For weeks, shouting, they'd tell her. At dinner. At breakfast. While she was in the bathroom.

She knew what they called her behind her back: Child of Satan. They talked about whether she might need an exorcist. While she snuck into the house with library books about witches and ghosts and E.S.P.

Worst of all, what if they followed her, stopped her, plucked her out of the bus like a rolling wayward grape, and said, "This is ours" ?

She knew that was what they believed. It was what she believed, deep down. She didn't want to hear it out loud. She was 18 only to the clock.

Not to them. Never to them.

And the RV giggled and groaned its way across America.

The Motel Room Speaks

Here they come, the latest transients, with their stained crumpled clothes and their whiny voices. Fumbling with the room key, slamming the door back into the wall likely as not (on the same caved-in spot), ready to complain about everything. So entitled they are. Before they even put their bags down they are wagging their heads around, looking for flaws.

"It's dark," they say first, as if this is unheard of at eleven o'clock at night. "Where's the damn switch?" It's exactly where it is supposed to be, but if they take five seconds finding it they are instantly aggrieved.

"Not much space, is there?" That's next. What do they expect for $60 a night? Room to do gymnastic routines? There is a table, two chairs, fairly new, I'll have you know, and a bed that is plenty wide for two human beings who are not too greedy. A bathroom. A TV. What more do you need for the next nine hours, eight of which you'll spend sleeping?

But oh, no! I'm not good enough for Mr. and Mrs. Slam, Bam, Thank you Ma'am! Where is the wi-fi, they want to know. As if nobody could live without it for one night on the way from point A to point B. You'd think they'd appreciate the rare chance to be incommunicado in a world with so little privacy.

It's always the same. The closet is "measly," there aren't enough drawers or hangers, and the bathroom! Oh, how they excoriate the bathroom. Too small, too noisy (what, you don't *want* a fan to dry things out?). Well, I don't like their musty odors clinging to the wall with the shower mist, either, just so you know! And don't get me started about the droop in the counter. How they go on about that. But I notice they always rest their own hips on it in the morning.

Look, very few surfaces are 100% level. And it's not my fault. It's the other fly-by-nighters, people no better than they, who lean on it, sit on it, set their overstuffed suitcases on it, even get carried away and have sloppy sex on it, if you can believe that. Oh, I've seen everything. It's so hypocritical. I didn't leave mildew in my own shower stall. I didn't pace the carpet bare or put cigarette holes in my own quilt. But who has to live with those flaws week after week, huh? And they'll be out of here at 10 tomorrow, probably bitching about having to check out so early. Yeah, suddenly they like me, and want to cling with sentimental fervor.

Enough of these day-trippers already, who leave their wet towels crumpled on the floor so the linoleum will curl up. You know what? I'm glad the walls are thin! Let them stay up all night listening to the threesome banging away next door. At least *they're* having fun.

A Toast to Opposites

Here's to the fresh start. Here's to the new room swept clean of debris. Here's to shelves with no dust on them. Here's to a place for everything and no excess. Here's to fresh energy, fresh colors, a room dewy with newness, like you are sitting in the middle of the forest.

Now, here's to the old and comfortable. All praise to the stained soft sweater that fits like skin and unravels over your knuckles. Here's to the desk piled high with familiar projects. There is joy in being able to find your things without looking, maybe even in the dark. There is sweetness in knowing things around you are unchanging, will not challenge you by suddenly demanding something different of you, maybe more than you have to offer.

Here's to the jump starters. The ones who say, "Let's get things going! Pull up that floor tile! Paint that cabinet! We're redecorating. Today!" Here's to being grabbed and shaken out of our routine, forced to face our own mess, eat our own dust, see with fresh eyes — catapulted out of our rut.

And now, here's to those who let us take our time. Here's to the kind souls who tiptoe by and let us finish our nap. Here's to friends who accept us as we are and don't complain about our bad breath. There is joy in letting our hair down. There is love in being allowed to do the same old stupid thing, the same old stupid way, until we decide for ourselves to change.

Here's to all things in their season.

The Assassins of May

The assassins of May are wardrobe assassins. To the guillotine with heavy sweaters! Death to all boots! It is not only Spring, it is almost Summer! To the Devil with cardigans! Who needs long sleeves?

Out come the gauzy scarves of summer, the spaghetti strap sundresses and the sandals and flip-flops. Off I trundle to the out-of-season closet, coats and jackets draped heavily over my forearm, long skirts trailing along the floor. They feel too warm even on my arm now, it is time for lightness! Aquas and corals and lemon and mint. White jeans, khakis, maybe crinkle cotton or even seersucker. No more knits! No more wool!

And no more hot chocolate or coffee, it is time for the kingdom of iced tea. Time for rocking on the front porch and watching the house cat stalk in the grass, while gently gossiping about one's neighbors. Time for hawks to build their yearly nest in the trees behind the yard. We will enjoy their silhouettes sweeping in to land, until the chicks are born and for months shriek their hunger unceasingly.

Time for walks in the afternoon, now, while it is warm instead of stifling. Time for light on water in the swimming pool before it glares. Time for the little pear tree, so much smaller than its neighbors and looking convincingly dead, to come forth with new shoots and even bounteous fruit buds, too early for the squirrels to snatch them. And oh, the days in the garden before the white-and-thin-skinned must retreat to air-conditioning and a shelf of much re-read favorite books. Spring, May and its assassins, is the time

for Celts: me & the little people, warming for just a stolen moment
outside our hollow hills.

Bag Lunch

Lucy huddled at the edge of the amphitheatre, watching the popular girls open their lunches.

"Yick, not bologna again," said Mara. She threw back her long, straight black hair and made a face.

The others looked vaguely sympathetic and unpacked their own meals. Lunchtime wasn't really about food; it was about being out of the classroom, gossiping, and flirting. It was a time to make sure everyone got a good look at your new camisole or lace-up boots.

Lucy munched morosely, looking at the others furtively. She soaked in their enjoyment, tried to imagine herself copying their gestures, their tones of voice. Lucy was plain, deeply overweight, and wore second hand clothes. Lucy's only pleasure in life was her grade card. For her, lunchtime was about food.

The girls were sharing side dishes and chattering.
"Want a slice of apple?"
"Ew, I hate pickles."
"I wish my mom would give me a Ho-Ho."

Lucy was silent. Nobody so much as glanced at her Italian meatball sandwich, dripping with sauce. Nothing of mine is desirable, thought Lucy simply, articulating to herself the unspoken.

Carla had condescended to invite her to join them for lunch, once Lucy agreed to loan her the biology class notes. But Carla did not find it necessary to talk to Lucy. One had one's standards, after all.

Sheila, the redhead with the heart shaped face, was offering peanut M 'n M's around from a large bag.

"Be care-ful, the green ones make you hor-ny," Maryellen chanted. It was just a reminder. Everyone knew that, though nobody knew where this piece of lore had originated. It was just one of those things that high school girls across the nation knew. The girls picked and pecked carefully from the bag.

Lucy was surprised when the bag appeared in her peripheral vision. She hadn't expected to be offered any.

"Would you like some?" the pretty redhead said politely.

Lucy looked sullenly at the crackly yellow bag. Maybe it was a trick. Sometimes that happened. They'd get a boy to ask her out in the hallway, say, then gather around and jeer when she said "yes."

"Hey, imagine if Lucy got horny," Mara snorted.
"Oh! My! God! The guys would all run away," Maryellen elaborated.
"She's too fat! It's not like she would catch them," Carla remarked scornfully.

Lucy looked at the ground. She could take some candy anyway. Or she could stand, lumbering, jiggling, and walk away in protest.

"I picked all the green ones out already," Sheila said softly. Her face remained open and smirkless, but there were little lines of displeasure around her lips. Sheila had always been nice, for a popular girl.

No matter what Lucy did, they would not respect her.

Lucy reached into the bag and grasped as much candy as she could, not even checking for color.

She ate.

What To Do with a Leaf
Julia's Story

It depends on the leaf, of course. If yours is young and green and swelling, just take it and run. Follow it anywhere. If it is yellow, see if you can pair it up with a gold, or a stunning crimson. If, like mine at the grand old age of 28, it is sere and crumpled, brown and crackly, dotted inside with spots where it has already died, it is time to turn it over for a new one.

Turning over a new leaf is all about reconsidering your choices. Especially choices you have dismissed before. When I went into rehab in 1985, I had long since decided that life without alcohol was not an option. It just hurt too much. Not only was I not going to try it, it wasn't even *possible*. It was only when life got very messy indeed, and the costs of blacking out got higher than I wanted to pay, that I started thinking again about living without a haze in my mind.

Living without haze meant I would feel everything, which meant life had to become less painful, which meant *everything* had to change. It all fell like dominoes. My career was one of the first casualties. It was as if booze was a brick wall I'd been beating my head against. When I stopped drinking, my head snapped through and I tumbled down the rabbit hole. Nothing was ever the same.

It was all better than advertised.

Cigarettes were similar. They were an emotional crutch that involved regular self-destruction. The payoff was feeling less, in a world still too piercing for me to tolerate. Again there was a choice: did I want to be fully conscious? Could I stand it? Could I even do it? There are people who cannot quit smoking even with a hole cut in their throats. Was I one of those? Did I even want to be a rudely healthy, righteous exerciser, climbing stairs and conquering treadmills? Wouldn't it be safer to cling to my bad-girl image? Was it even possible to sit and ponder life quietly without wisps of warm grey smoke trickling out of my mouth?

Ultimately changing has always been about facing things I haven't looked squarely in the eye; walking into the wind instead of hiding behind the nearest boulder. Feeling the onslaught of full-sized emotions like a tidal wave, standing still for that, and coming out drenched and gasping on the other side.

Does life always reward you when you do this? I don't know. My life has gotten immensely easier, but is it that way for everybody?

What I have discovered, over and over, is that I have more choices than I think.

When I run down the alley in the dark, with the bad guys behind me, and hit a dead end, the thing to do is head back toward the danger – just for a minute – and reconsider some of those exits I passed.

Because somewhere out there, there is a bigger street, a city, a life.

If I don't just huddle at the dead end, I can get away — and leave those bad guys muttering, *Curses, foiled again!*

In the Dark

Cassie sat in the closet and thought about the dark. It occurred to her she was always in the dark anyway. Not just the clingy dark of her bedroom at night, but the dark of time.

She thought about time as being like the closet. It was full of stuff, like cleaning supplies and useful rags and recyclable bags and linens and fluffy towels, fancy for guests and old stringy ones for her and Ed. She knew they were there. But she couldn't see anything except vague shapes right now, with the door closed. You could imagine almost anything, stacked up on the shelf liners. The mop on the corner with the strings hanging upside down in the air could be a human head, coming to get you. And time was a little like that, at least the future was. You couldn't see what was coming, ever. You might think you knew; you might have an idea. But you couldn't clearly see what was around you, ready to fall on your head if you made a wrong move.

If you tried anything, you might find out. It might be just the same old familiar things you bump against; or it might be monsters or something worse. It might be something you only thought was familiar, twisted into a horrible new shape as it lunged out of the shadows at you.

That's why we don't want to move, she thought, running her fingers over and over through the shag rug. We're afraid it will all come tumbling down around us if we get up on wobbly feet and lurch around. The blackness will pelt us with cans and broomsticks and sticky things that trail down over our arms. They had a place to be, but then we moved and disturbed everything.

That's why she'd put up with Ed so long. She'd always been kind of in the dark about what they were doing together, why it lasted, where it was going. But as long as she was safe and still, tucked against the bedsheets, not disturbing anything, she didn't need to know.

I would be happy to stay in the dark, Cassie thought. As long as I stay here, I don't have to walk in on the two of them, screwing on my bed like I don't exist. It's better this way. I don't have to face the future, where we'll all have to think of something to say to each other.

We'll all have to see what we've been doing.

Fountains

There were fountains all over the house. Two in the living room. One each in the dining and bedroom. Two more in the study. Even one in the bathroom. Wherever one sat in the house, one could hear water doing something; rippling or soothing or trilling or cycling. It covered a multitude of sins. It also disappeared into the background after a while. Denise would look up from a book, notice the rush of liquid, and realize she hadn't consciously heard it in days.

It was one of his little oddities. He just liked fountains. Every so often she would catch him looking at more on eBay. "Well, we don't have one in the kitchen," he'd say sheepishly. He was a quiet, humble man; didn't speak much, didn't ask for much. She let him have his multiple fountains, and never complained as she replenished and cleaned and polished them, scrubbing the green dye off the one with colored water. The water left spots all around.

Before dawn one morning Denise woke from one of her nightmares. As she tried to calm her nerves, hoping not to wake him, she noticed a distant chatter and hush. It sounded like somebody speaking just out of earshot. Then she realized that someone *was* talking: it was her husband, soothing her with the bubble and flow, even though he was asleep. They were there to speak for him. They said, *You are safe. You are here with me in our home, and I love you.*

He was a quiet man. But he spoke in many languages.

Snake

It seems so petty, but I have a headache. Weren't those minor characters in old romances always contracting headaches and retiring to bed for the whole afternoon? A maid would sit with them and soothe them by dabbing their temples with lavender water. Who knows what the maid felt, waiting on her as the lady sniffed and complained in a die-away voice that she would rather be playing croquet on the lawn, or walking in the Conservatory with Theodore? The maid wasn't even allowed in the Conservatory, probably. If I were her, I'd have a headache too, just listening to all of that aristocratic self-pity.

They would fake their headaches too, those ladies, when they didn't want to face something. Is Robby the Ravisher waiting for you, leering over a bouquet of violets in your parlor? Ah, you cannot see him – you have the headache! Is Mama making an unpleasant scene because you rode out with Lord Pevensey in his closed barouche without a chaperone? Please, Mama, I must be excused, I have developed the most dreadful headache!

Having a headache meant one could do nothing – nothing at all – not even those few proper things allowed to a lady of good family.

So, enough of being a lady! I think I'll shed my clothes and my skin and shimmy down out of this headache and out of womanness and onto the forest floor. I will become a snake instead. I will wiggle into the dry leaves and compost and scurrying bugs. I will swing everything side to side – not just my hips, I will have no hips – and wobble, like a wave approaching the beach on a moonless night. Down through all the debris beneath the trees: twigs and rotted fallen things, left-behind apple cores and all the less mentionable bits one finds in murky, secret places. Things that a proper Victorian lady should not know about, or if she knows, should never mention.

Being a snake suits me. You can think what you want when you're a snake. Those precious ladies have so many headaches only because of all those things they're not allowed to think. Those unsanctioned thoughts build up behind their brows and press and burn and send them to bed.

That sort of lady jumps and shivers when she sees a snake. She sees that bullet shaped nose, those hard black blinkless eyes, and she knows that the snake might be thinking of anything, anything at all. It worries her, what the snake might be thinking of all unsanctioned. Even if the snake says nothing. She knows that if the snake spoke, it would tell her things she doesn't want to know, is not allowed to know.

I remember when I was a snake before, once, long ago. I made the mistake of speaking, in those days. There weren't very many women then, and they didn't wear much. But even then, they had to watch what they were thinking.

I told one of them – I forget why I bothered with her – that she ought to reconsider her choices. Why was the world in her head so small? Why didn't she think what she liked? She said it was God's idea, and one mustn't argue with God. She said thinking brought knowledge, and the fruit of the tree of knowledge was forbidden.

I said that she needed to rethink her God. She said she had a headache, and went away.

Yes, I like being a snake. I think I'll stay this way. Being a woman is much too hard. I can't see the point, really.

Slinking in the muck is more fun. You go where you want, you think what you like, and no one follows you into the dusky, unhallowed places.

I won't talk to women any more, though. People don't like it when you tell them about the things they're refusing to think. Once they think about these things, they must act. Then whatever they do, it is somehow the snake's fault for telling them the truth.

Snakes have a bad rap. But we don't care.

Hiding

Chastity was in the pantry. She was on the third shelf, behind the canned tomatoes. It was the wrong season, there were lots of fresh tomatoes, nobody would be looking for canned. They were looking for her, but they wouldn't look here.

Chastity was five, and Daddy was angry. She didn't know what it was about. She just knew he wanted all the children, now, and she knew what that meant.

Someone had done something wrong, and Daddy didn't know who. So he would line them all up and make them tell on each other. If nobody told, they would ALL get spanked, not just the guilty one. It worked every time.

Chastity didn't like being spanked with the flat wooden paddle – or worse, with the belt, if he was really mad – but that didn't make her hide. After all, she would be spanked for hiding, too.

What she hated was everybody being spanked in front of each other. She hated their tortured humiliated faces, trying not to cry when their pants were pulled down and everybody was looking. It was even worse if someone confessed, or somebody told on someone else. Then one was spanked alone, cried and whimpered alone, and stood gulping while Daddy lectured on badness, and evil, and honesty, and praised the one who had told. But the one who told was breathing fast and feeling queasy, getting smaller and smaller inside, worthless and faceless as a potato to the other children.

What was it this time? Walnut shells broken on the garage floor? Or the flashlight missing? Or a bottle of spilled milk? She couldn't think of anything wrong; no pranks, no disobedience. It must be something little, this time. Maybe something nobody knew they did.

You never knew if Daddy would get mad at the little things or the big things, or not mad at anything. Some days he was like that. Some days he yelled if the phone rang during dinner time, shrieking "Leave me alone!!" Other times he came home happy and took off his tie and got on the floor and pretended he was a lion. You could climb all over him then, and tickle and choke him, and he would not mind.

Some days it was only grownups he got mad at. Those were the days when Momma hid behind the ferns. Chastity knew, but she didn't say anything. If she told anyone else, they might give it away.

She heard yelps and crying from the living room now. All the kids were crying. Only one was yelping. So someone had snitched.

If she waited awhile, Daddy would calm down. Maybe he would just frown, but stop turning purple and red. It was scary when he did that. That's when you worried you would get hurt.

But if he just frowned, and used his hand and not a paddle, it would not be so bad. And not in front of the boys, *Please*.

She shifted on her squatting legs, hoping her foot would not fall asleep.

Daddy was lecturing now. She could hear his voice rise and drone and peak and drone again. It might be a long wait.

She wondered if she would get dinner tonight.

It's Complicated

Marissa took a swallow of coffee and leaned back in her chair. "So that's it for me. What's new with you? I heard you've been married a couple years now. Tell me!"

Shelley shifted her coffee cup around in a little circle on the table. Her cinnamon brows were crooked beneath her bangs. "He was just a one night stand, to begin with," she said slowly. "You know, you see a handsome guy at the movies, you're alone, you have nothing to do, so at intermission you flirt. Get him to light your cigarette, that kind of thing. He takes you home, next day he says 'I'll call you,' and that's that. No muss, no fuss.

"Except he did call back. I was so surprised. And he was so nice, and so good looking, and he kept asking me out, and pretty soon he was really my boyfriend."

"Sounds promising," Marissa smiled.

Shelley raised her eyebrows. "I thought so! And then one day, out of the blue, he said he couldn't see me anymore because he was getting married."

"What! So he'd been seeing someone else."

"Not exactly…he had this female friend who had been abandoned by her lover just when she discovered she was pregnant. And my boyfriend had a student visa that was up, and didn't dare go back to his own country. He told me Iranians were returning from America and just disappearing off the pavement at the airport – never seen again.

"So he figured he'd solve both their problems by marrying her."

"Did you know about any of this?"

"Unh-unh. And actually it would have been okay, we weren't committed or anything, except as soon as he left I realized I was desperately in love and couldn't stand to lose him. I decided if he had to marry someone, it should be me! So I started sending him roses – one the first day, two the second day, then three and so forth. The plan was to go up to 10 and then with the tenth send a note for the first time and it would say, 'I love you'."

"Well, it must have worked, since you're married now."

"No. The third day he called and asked me to please stop. It made him feel bad."

"So then what?"

"I told him I was pregnant." She looked away.

Marissa almost jumped from her seat. "You have a kid? No one told me that!"

"Um. No. I just said that to get him to leave her. I was so insane, Marissa. I used to park in the driveway across from his house at night and wait for his shadow to fall on the blinds. I pined and prayed and starved myself down to 90 pounds and had daydreams about poisoning her. I totally was ready to say anything, and I didn't think for a second what I would do when there really wasn't any baby.

"But it didn't work. He said he was committed to this partnership with his friend and he couldn't back out now."

"Wait. You *are* married to this guy, right?"

"Yup. Two years tomorrow."

"So what happened?"

"I gave up. I went into this total depression. Then one night he called out of nowhere. He said the girl's old boyfriend had come around and said he'd take her back! So he had to get an annulment, but after that he was free again, and he still needed to get married. So that's how it went down. We went to Carson City that September and stood up in front of a judge and his secretary."

"Geez. What a story. So now you're settled." Marissa sat back and smiled.

Shelley put her coffee cup down and bunched her fingers on the table. They looked very white and cold. "Not exactly. I want a divorce. See there's this guy…"

Cycle Suit — A Tribute

My husband has a special suit for bicycling. It is navy blue, of some stretchy fabric that wicks moisture away from his body. There is a short-sleeved top which zips up the front to a mandarin collar. The shorts are tight, and run halfway down his thighs. There are advertising patches and slogans all over this shirt: UPS and Federal Express and STP and god knows what, all in red, white and blue. It is the only time you will ever find him advertising anything.

To him, the suit is merely practical, with its catchall back pocket. There are matching gloves for grasping the handlebars; narrow, racer-type shoes with spikes on the bottom that curve precisely into the holes on his foot pedals.

But to me, it is the only time he gives himself away.

He spends his days disguised as an ordinary man. He says little, listens much, and walks quietly in nondescript jeans and T-shirt. In his bike suit, he is revealed for the erotic animal that he is. This is a body long-limbed and finely tuned. This is a flat stomach at the age of 65, and a head full of gleaming, slightly wavy blonde hair. This is a trim waist rising to just-broad-enough shoulders with beautiful, easy posture, and casually strong arms and hands from decades of professional drumming. The little curly hairs on his endless legs gleam in the sun, his calves tensile and curved. A Hermes-like body — the best kept secret in local dating circles.

Years of disciplined exercise have made his body rocklike. On holidays, for fun, he cycles up to the top of Mount Diablo (no, I do not go with him!).

But I have a photo of him at the top, so pleased with himself that he has released his smile, his other precious secret. It raises his face from good looking to celebrity handsome. When I see his eyes tilt up, his lips open on joy, I feel like a child whose mother let her take off the scratchy bathing suit and run into the waves on a beach. I feel like I have been given a trunk full of treasure, just to run my fingers through.

My movie star. My quiet husband, who never flirted in his life, and usually couldn't get a second date. And found me, when I had given up.

Next

The word 'next' can be a weary one. It can be part of an achingly long line of numbers at the DMV or at the doctor's. The room is full. It is a hot day; the air is thick and no one is moving, except to wave listlessly at a horsefly which is doing a tepid ballet in everyone's face by turns. The seats are vinyl, and your thighs are sweating. The nurse or clerk pretends she is going to meet somebody's eye. But she hasn't done that since 10 A.M., which is the last time anyone felt like a fellow human to her. She says it, as she has said it for hours, hopelessly, that awful word, "Next." And it is as if she is reading a horror story: as if you were underwater, drowning, waiting your turn for just one breath of air, and what you hear instead of 'next' is 'Nevermore.'

Or the word 'next' can be a childish one, full of excitement: Christmas Day when you are five, and the gifts are tumbling glossily over each other like a mound of puppies. Each one is delightful. Each one is wriggling for attention. And your parents say, "Go ahead. Which one do you want to open *next?*"

But for Nancy, 'next' carried a frisson of fear, a sense of jazzed dread. It was as if she was running up a hill, away from pursuing hounds with their mouths open and tongues perspiring moistly over grinding sepia teeth. She knew it was possible to win this race, to outdistance or trick them and come out at Valhalla, gloriously replete and free. But it was also possible to die horribly halfway there, a prey that wasn't challenge enough, that might not be tasty enough, that might just be left alone to die of its wounds after a little cranky mauling.

Nancy had reached the top of the hill, so to speak. He was taking her out somewhere special; he was going to ask her to marry him, she just knew it; she could leave this poverty behind and live in a house instead of a ghetto, with a hot tub and two cars. More than that, she could be loved forever by a good man, which was the only thing she had ever wanted out of life. The house was just icing.

Or she could be alone in her accustomed despair. Forever.

She was just far enough ahead; she had just enough breath. She could plunge down into a stream and a forest and lose the pursuing dogs of isolation and poverty, or she could come face to face with a rough granite wall, trapped for their cunning jaws. It all depended on what came next.

She had come from utter despair. She had come from the waiting-room 'next.' She had absolutely nothing to go back to. She knew what the jaws of those dogs felt like. She had been left for dead on the mountain more than once.

But she had everything to gain. She had never been to Valhalla: she never had the ticket of entry before. You only get one chance and she is running, running as she has never run because it was never this worthwhile before, using every bit of breath she has. She doesn't know if it will be enough.

But if she has enough heart, if she finds enough speed, what's next will be the only next she will ever need.

Not Pictured Here

In the photo, you can't really tell what you're looking at. That's partly because it was taken with a phone camera. I am a poor photographer with the best of equipment, and this was not the best. It's blurred, too. My hand moved. It was just some poet standing up to read, anyway. I think even as I snapped the button, I knew that what I truly wanted to see could not be caught on film.

It was Vampyre Mike's wake. I walked in an hour late in any case. Finding parking in that neighborhood took a full hour; but also I had started late because I had my doubts about the wakes of poets and their value.

Poets do not come just to mourn and glorify their dead: they come to show off their poetry. They come to show how intimate they were with the deceased, and especially to disparage or pity or gloat if they had an affair with the dead. Some get dishonest and sappy, as bad as any church eulogy. Others write five pages of doggerel and can pass it off because it's 'grieving.' Perhaps by the end listeners will realize you only had lunch with him once in your life. People read poems who didn't even know the deceased, and say so.

So I arrived late, doubtfully, and past the point where the crowd was paying attention. I read second to last, which was about what I expected. My piece was only a few lines long, and I didn't mention our brief affair, decades ago.

Michael had been around forever among the SF poets. He always wore black from head to toe, had a cynical, grating voice, and in later years a slight tic that looked like a wink. He claimed to be a vampire. He even had a coffin. He kept it at Chris Trian's house, though, since his personal hole at the residence hotel at the end of Lombard Street was too small. He claimed this hotel had ghosts and wrote about them. I never saw them, and I never knew if what he wrote was what he had seen, or a story. He wrote funny, debauched poems that emphasized how absurd and horrible life is, and how nobody cares. He smoked. For a number of years, he drank devotedly. He had hepatitis C, but that's not what killed him.

All of it was a front. Oh, not that he didn't believe life was horrible and the wicked would triumph. He did. But what I found out by spending time with Mike was that he had a marshmallow heart. He drank because life hurt too much. Life hurt too much because he cared.

I remember standing crammed in the hallway of Café Babar's back room next to Mike and suddenly hearing that Paul Landry had died. First shock, then tears. I thought he had more time. I had planned to visit him. I turned and hid my forehead in Mike's scuffed and smoky black leather jacket. He tucked me under his chin and kissed the top of my head. I don't know if anyone else was crying. I didn't look up. Mike didn't say a word, and we never discussed it afterward.

I didn't read at Paul Landry's wake, I barely read at Mike's, and nobody remembers that I did. I almost didn't go. I almost didn't take the picture. What was the point? He wasn't going to be in it.

Dear Corner Couch,

Given that I have been monopolizing your attention for years, perhaps I should declare myself.

I love you. I love your coziness, sheltered at my back by a wall, and on the side by a loveseat. This makes me feel cradled and safe. No one can creep up on me, look over my shoulder, or disturb me. I love how I can cuddle up on the arm of the couch and still have room to stretch out my legs if I'm sleepy. I love the panoramic view of our living room, the window to the backyard, looking out on my shady nook with the honeysuckle vines. I can overlook my whole life from where I sit.

Everything I need is in reach. The coffee table, the trash can, and my big basket with all my creative supplies. So much to play with! Pens and extra journals, sketchpad, embroidery kit, bead working kit, watercolor kit, pastels – never mind that I never use them! They are available, if I actually gave myself permission to have fun. My iPad lives there, which is really a mini desk. My husband puts the U.S. Mail here. I bring my sewing to you, Mr Corner, I watch movies and listen to music here, and there have even been several intimate events. Really I spend more time with you than I actually spend with my husband.

Most of all, I read here with you, at all hours of the day and night, almost to the point of addiction. This disturbs me.

I am disturbed by several things in our relationship. The jealousy, for instance. I find myself quite offended these days if anyone spends a few minutes with you. I am worried about the way we linger hour after hour, even when I should be doing other things.

Sometimes I stay with you when I should be elsewhere. Surely our love should be a little less exclusive?

Have we become too comfortable, being silent together?

You have reshaped yourself to fit me. A girlfriend told me the other day that she could not remember ever seeing me anywhere else. This gave me pause. I think perhaps we need a little space. I think it might be time to see other people. It might be a good idea for me to leave the room more often. There are other couches, other rooms – I am coming to believe I should leave the house altogether on occasion, find other sources of comfort.

Not that I would abandon you. No, never. But it is time for some openness and variety in our association. I hope you understand.

You will always be my First Couch.

Yours Sincerely,

Saint Patrick's Day Reverie

Consider the potato. This potato. A potato with a purplish skin like an onion. Small and curvy, with dimples, like a smiling girl child. But no girl could get away with six or seven dimples, as this potato does, and still look appealing. It does not make one think of food. It looks more like an art object, egg like, cool and balanced.

I can imagine it sitting on the shelf of a glossy black étagère, with a docent walking by, intoning, "Exhibit Number Five, The Potato. The potato, ladies and gentlemen, is the history of Ireland." I think of the way so many thousands died for lack of them. Of the way Ireland used to be more crowded than India, according to observers of that century. Poverty there like no other poverty on earth. Tiny handkerchief fields that yielded only potatoes, divided and subdivided among sons until each one got only one row, or two, a few inches from the next subdivision.

I think of how people who starved grew heavy, overlong hair on their arms as their bodies tried to compensate for the temperature drop of no fat. Girls with anorexia still do that today. Back then, the starving would see this and other strange bodily mutations, and be repulsed and swept by rage and then apathy, since there was no fuel to feed the energy of rage. All for a potato.

And what did Ireland eat before potatoes? Surely there was a time when crops, poor and ill-drained as they must have been, would have been different, more various? Back in the days when the Celts had their own gods, many of them female; and marriages were contracted five years at a time, like term life insurance, with a pre-arranged distribution of sod hut and fields and sheep, if the contracts were not renewed. Back before the Celts and the Britons

33

were a wholly different people, inimical to each other. Back before the Pope swept his hand over the map and declared that Ireland was "granted" to England as a possession, like a barn or an extra dress.

What was it, to be in those Pre-Christian times? Back in the days when religion was tied to the earth, not to mankind, and humans could look at a tree and understand that it was holy?

In the end, the Papal God subsumed Bridget, and took over the hearts of the whole country – and then the Papal God itself was subsumed by the Church of England, and suddenly being Catholic was a good enough reason to despise an Irishman, refuse him property and rights, make his life hell.

I remember when Ireland's terrorism was a recurring boil on the face of politics, as recalcitrant as Jerusalem. I wondered if the bombings could ever stop. And then one year I looked again, and saw that while I'd glanced away the whole mess had been more or less resolved. There was a peaceful republic toddling along, not very profitable but stolid, taking in tourists, asking every customer at every meal, "Do you want 'taties with that?" Still the same food source, after it all.

We want to count on what we've always counted on. We do not like to change our form of nourishment. I think of this as I turn day after day to my books and my husband, ignoring the other things life offers, cold-shouldering the inevitable day when my husband will die and my eyes will fail and my heart, not open to other pleasures, turns to the wall and starves.

Snapshot: Madness in the Middle Classes

If you look in from the outside, you can't tell what's the matter. The woman is crying, but she's crying in a beautiful garden with jasmine trailing down the column behind her. You can just see a hummingbird, if you look carefully at that top right shadow. The woman is well dressed, the sky is blue, and it appears this is a pleasant Spring or Summer day. She is comfortably seated on a redwood chair, and the man leaning over her shoulder looks both concerned and attractive. In the background is a spacious white house. On the table are lovely fruits – melons and cantaloupe and grapes, cut up in wooden bowls, with a pitcher of water nearby; and you just know that pitcher is cold and the water tastes of squeezed lemon.

If you are cold, if you are hungry, if you are homeless or lonely, you will have no sympathy for this woman. Surely, you think, if I could be surrounded by love and abundance, I would not be sitting with puffy red eyes and a mound of wadded Kleenex in front of me.

And in truth, the woman is grateful. She knows how lucky she is. She knows she has everything others strive for all their lives and do not get. She knows it would all be worse if she were alone, if she were dirty and cold, if no one cared. Nevertheless, she is in pain, and when you are in pain, nothing else matters.

Pain is the greatest single feature in any landscape. It is like a mountain of burning granite, so large you cannot see around it or even up to the top, and so hot you cannot escape its radiating presence even if you turn your back. Pain is a mountain that has no path, no matter how many times you have climbed it. Pain is the place you must go alone, even if you are surrounded by friends.

Maybe you had a good reason for climbing the pain mountain. Maybe it was logical and imperative and inspired. But no matter how much you believe in your quest, the further up the mountain the less sense it will make. As the air grows broiling and unbreathable, you will wonder why you came. Before you reach the peak of pain, you might realize that it was not worth it; nothing could be worse than the pike in your heart, the fire of the rocks on the bare flesh of your feet. Reaching the top is pointless, but turning around to go down will be just as bad. The only real way out is to die here. Some people do.

This woman's mountain is mental illness. The pain works its way into her brain without reason or warning. She has no idea why she is climbing this mountain. She knows that if she lives to return, no one will be surprised or congratulate her. They assume she will not die up there. She never has before. They assume it cannot be that hard. They assume there must be a good reason. They don't understand that insanity doesn't have to have a reason.

They do not have this particular mountain in their country.

The woman takes another pill and after half hour or so, starts climbing slowly down the mountain, back to where she started. She will not arrive at the farther side. She will not be further along on her path. She sees the man waiting for her. She hears him say, 'I love you.' She is dimly aware of the garden at the bottom and the warm bed with the clean sheets. She will be free of the pain. If she just hangs on a little longer.

But it will only be a rest stop. She will have to climb this mountain again, maybe as soon as tomorrow. It will happen all over and nothing will change. And she cannot bring home the truth she found at the top – that this is not worth it, that it doesn't matter, it never matters, the beauty of the country wherein you suffer. She will come down with the truth in her pocket and show it to no one. She will never be allowed to stop on the mountaintop and die.

Because she promised him. She promised she would always come home.

Mother's Dress

There was a dress her mother wore which was almost mystical. Only now can she articulate what happened when Mother wore it: she turned into the Eternal Feminine Principal, come to life and swiveling many times the girl's size (as all goddesses must be) in the glamorous three-way mirror.

It was a gown that moved like smoke. The color was a dusky taupe that edged on brown but didn't quite go all the way there. Above this pleated, floating border, the color faded and blanched into silhouettes of trees that stood sentinel all the way around her, defining her thighs. The girl thinks now that they were oaks, and remembers that the oak was sacred to Druids, the people from whom she descended. Above these trees, smoke hues returned again and were cinched in at her Mother's dark waist, with a belt that pulled that area to its tiniest circumference. The bodice rode up her body in neat hugging lines to short, squared sleeves.

Her mother in this memory can't be more than 22, and she has dewy perfection of a kind she is not to own much longer. The girl has three small brothers at this point, all under five years, and they have not broken her Mother; it takes the final baby and a grueling move to do that. In the next house, there is no landscaping; her father and mother mix cement and carry loads of rock, and sweat, and she catches her first glimpse of the woman she will know later. Outdated garish pants, hair standing up, and lines of semi-permanent downward displeasure. She does not smell good. She does not wear socks. She is too far from the radiant lady in a sleek chignon. The girl is too close to teenaged, judgemental, and for the first time she thinks, *I don't want to look like her*. For the first time, she wonders what possessed her mother to wear red plaid pants, and she gripes that she should not have to take care of babies and fix lunch while mother sweats and frowns. The goddess has fallen, if not all the way down, at least knocked to one knee for the count.

But at 22, her mother is the embodiment of glamour. Her fingernails are peerless ovals, not like the girl's stubby digits, and her arms pouring out of the small sleeves embody why they were once called "limbs," and hidden away from men's desire. Her clothes are still fairly new; her husband still takes her on dates; her stomach is still flat, her curves in beautiful proportion. And the girl goes into a trance watching her Mother smooth the slip under the wraithlike dress. She thinks, *Someday, this is what I will be.*

But it never happens, and whenever she looks in the mirror she sees her Mother behind her, like smoke, and the girl's face looks plain. The word she wants, to describe that vanished time, is an old one: worship. And once it passes, it does not return.

The Shadow

She stands in the mosque in Tehran. The call to prayer is long past; other women have filtered out, chatting in low voices behind their *chador*. She cannot speak from behind that black prison over her mouth. She knows they don't want her to talk, that's why the cloth is there, to muffle her, like an explosion. She has been in the city under the stifling black band for two weeks, and already she feels smaller, denser, less visible: she is gathering for an explosion.

This was supposed to be a vacation, but it is a nightmare of heat and suppression. She feels as if the whole subtext of civilization has risen up through the sand and proven to be a creature that only eats women, preferably virgins. But it takes its time digesting them. She wants to think she is indigestible, but fears she is not. Given time, would she too dissolve in their indifference, and become just another black cotton hole in the landscape? A shadow in a land where light rules everything.

She drops her head and swerves toward the exit to the women's section, but there is a darkness in the archway, and it is male. She can see the outline, a proud Eastern nose never to be mistaken for a European profile. He is hovering there.

She thinks suddenly of the ex-husband she married so blithely in her twenties. She was nubile then, energetic and convinced that cultural differences would bow down to love. What if it were he in the doorway? He was from this area, and after their divorce, he had returned home.

She has always thought there were things unfinished between them, some agreement that should have been reached. For a moment, dizzy in the heat, she fantasizes that he will come into the light and finally say, *I am sorry I made you cry and wait for 48 hours for me to come home from 'a walk.' I know you said that I hated for you to have fun, that I couldn't tolerate your smile. It is because my mother never smiled – how could she, behind the veil? My mother never went to the movies, or to the bazaar with money of her own, or out dancing in bright colors, so how could you? I left you in silence and anger,* he'd say. *But then I came home and saw what we'd done to my mother, what we'd done to all of them. I understood that my bride from now on would be black cloth and a bended head. I understood what you'd been trying to say.*

The man shifts into the light, and it is no one she knows. She gulps air and brushes past him, cringing away from the dusty cloth of his tunic, afraid to touch and be contaminated, contained.

In her pocket she clutches her passport. She leaves the mosque. She does not belong here. She will go back to the hotel and tear off this hateful *chador*, she will cross her legs in a pencil skirt, she will light a cigarette. They will see that she does not belong here. She cannot be contained like that. Surely she is visible. Anyone can see that, anyone at all.

Can't they?

All the Underwear

There had been a time when she was always alone. Alone at work, cut off from the girls in the other cubicles by her artist's attitude and her conviction that neither work nor money was a life. Alone on the bus, bumping irregularly down vague grey-block streets to her grey-block apartment, carrying too many totes and books in bright colors that wanted to wriggle out of her arms like restless baby pigs. Alone in her apartment, lying down on the thin pull-out bed, exhausted at 7 o'clock by nothingness; waiting patiently for the sky to darken and give her official permission for unconsciousness.

Alone at the movies. Alone in the thrift store. Alone in the maze of her mind, where thoughts echoed, like sound, in the emptiness; she found her way to conclusions sonically, like a bat.

There had been peculiar compensations. No one to explain to, ever. No need to justify any action she chose. Her points of view were unchallenged, and thus obviously right. She moved on her own schedule, she stayed in bed if she wanted; eating things that left crumbs on the sheets if she pleased. She could sing out loud, silly songs that were only funny to her, and make cow noises. In her tiny studio, she was as free as a woman could possibly be.

Some nights she padded about naked, or danced on the bed to very loud music with a cucumber as a microphone, playing the same favorite song over and over. Or she would pretend she was out in a field, in the middle of a fruiting pumpkin patch, bare-breasted and lashing her hair wildly about.

But are you truly naked when there is no one to notice and be shocked? When you finish painting a room that no one sees, has it changed color?

Now, married, she was never alone, even in sleep. Now she could wake from a nightmare and find her husband there, (no mandibles, tentacles, or extra arms) ready to hold her and whisper into her hair. Even when he left for the day, she looked forward to him returning, seeing what she'd done with her day. She rehearsed how she'd relate her achievements. He would see it all – if she had made the bed, picked up her clothes, watered the lawn, done the laundry. Oh, god, the laundry! It was never done (he was a hard-laboring, sweaty guy; his clothes went to the wash every day. She was sedentary and dry; 9 times out of 10 she sniffed hers and hung them back up).

Some days she wished to revert to sonic echoes. But there was always his underwear to pick up, the mail to distribute, the dog to feed, the dishes. These things nailed her to her day and kept her getting up even if the day seemed unworthy. It was a fair tradeoff. There would be no more dancing naked without an audience. But there would be no more black Saturdays lying 12 hours on a mattress.

She had an anonymous photo in her study – she had a study! A bedroom, a garbage disposal, an ice-maker! As I say, a picture in her very own study, a picture of which she did not know the origins. It was a black and white of a very mature couple. They were looking at the camera with arms around each other's shoulders. You almost couldn't tell, anymore, which was the woman and which was the man, as they returned to blessed androgyny. It appeared that one had a less reliable spine than the other. Yet it was not clear who was supporting whom. There was a shine in their eyes she had never seen in younger people's: the successful shedding of the ego, the nearness to merging at last.

For that, if she could get it, she would pick up all the underwear there was.

Do You Hear That?

I seceded from my family at about 12 years of age. It was sort of a mutual thing. For a variety of reasons, such as me liking no one, I had become a person no one liked. I ended up one very silent teenager lying on her bed with a gaming console for six years straight.

Communion with my family was only what I heard through the walls. Mine was the only downstairs bedroom, next door to the television room. By day, I would hear their muffled game shows and serials, their arguments over channels, and the sounds of imminent dinner (the only occasion for which I actually appeared in person). At night I would hear tussles and toilets overhead, the last door slamming, a creak of bedsprings, and maybe one final set of small feet pattering to the bathroom. Soon all would be quiet except for the sounds of my parents' pillow talk, muted through the ceiling.

I cannot tell you how safe those bass and alto melodies made me feel. They wound around each other in mellow rings. No matter what the squabbles of the day, after the lights went out, my parents agreed, and sounded wise. They floated above my head like God plotting, deciding who we would be. And even if I didn't agree, what security there was in knowing that in their combined adult knowledge, they were planning. We were not adrift.

Nevertheless. I was young, I knew everything, I didn't need them, and I couldn't wait to get out of there.

Two weeks after I was 18, I graduated from house sounds to dormitory noises— blow dryers at six in the morning, because god knows it takes hours to get your hair right when you're young — closet doors zipping to and fro on their runners and pots clinking in the tiny kitchen down the hall. During the day I listened to the drone of professors and the whispering of students. I still stayed in my room all the time. But now it was legitimate, I was studying. The ones who stayed up late giggling together got bad grades. I snubbed them.

And now, at last, I have my own apartment. It is quiet. The TV which I never watch is silent in the corner. No one cooks or chatters or sings or argues, and the telephone never rings. It is what I always wanted. Perfect peace. But late at night, I dig deeper into my book with a sort of desperation.

Do you hear that?

It is the sound of no one caring.

Bus to Nowhere

She looked out the window. The view was blurred and bumpy, cut in half by the heavy metal sash, jerking along as the bus rattled and coughed and dropped into potholes along the way. The road was beginning to be more pothole than pavement as they wound deeper into the countryside.

The windows weren't well sealed. Overnight the dust outside had seeped into the groove of the window and between her teeth. It didn't make things worse,   since she hadn't brushed since she boarded. No matter what, her mouth was going to taste terrible. She had eaten various nameless snacks and some tamales at the rest stops. She was vaguely disturbed at the thought of food particles decomposing in her mouth. Somehow the dust seemed to balance things out, as if the dry grit would keep her mouth from rotting. *I'd prefer my teeth don't rot, even if my mind does.*

She rearranged the purse in her lap and rested her forehead on the glass. There was nothing to see, but she didn't want to, anyway. Dust and powdered rocks and occasional muted trees were just fine with her. Shacks hove into view from time to time, peopled with unsupervised brown children playing listlessly in the weeds. Once there had been an adult, too, but he was so limp and sprawled he looked unconscious —or dead. It was hard to tell beneath the sombrero.

Nobody tried to talk to her. She was left to herself as the *mamacitas* pulled out baskets and tote bags and towel-wrapped foods. She tried not to understand anything they said. After all, people's problems were the same everywhere. Why hear it again? Why pretend she had answers or dregs of compassion?

The couple in the back droned on with their low, tight-voiced argument. They thought they were in love, they thought it was important, that pushing and pulling at each other with words would bring them to some new place where they would like each other better. They'd been arguing since they got on, but it hadn't happened yet.

Hard to ignore the chickens, though. They seemed incapable of settling into their crates. Once a hen had pecked a slat loose and come hunting for grubs and trash under the seats. She was rust and black and white, more colorful than the sandy terrain or the grey vegetation.

The bus driver had tried arguing with her at first in broken English. She did not want this bus, no, it went noplace, no city, no ruins, no hotels. It wasn't clear where it did go, except away from the coast and to the end of some remote line she could not pronounce. That's where she was going, to the end of the line.

Because she understood, at last, that she already lived there.

Downhill

Things tend to run downhill. Water, avalanches, tennis balls, cars that won't start, relationships and love affairs. At the bottom of the hill, things usually end. Think about it: how many people quit at the peak of an affair, just when every date is terrific and every glance fizzes like champagne? No, you quit when things hit bottom — and they always do, because implied in the word 'peak' is the flatland or valley without which there are no heights.

Things run downhill. The peak lasts only a moment. The air is too thin up there, the effort too intense to maintain. And the slope downward is not a bad thing. Think of a bicycle ride, of the clean sweep of wind past your ears. Think of the smooth drop of a skateboard or a slide. Think of the easy familiarity of an accustomed love, with whom you can take off your shoes and prop up your feet. Down is not a bad direction.

Things run downhill, or break apart and tumble, and when they hit bottom, they rock or roll around a while, sometimes a very long while indeed, like an ugly lawsuit. As long as there is striving, as long as one still believes that up is the only direction, that the heights can be reached again, the dust refuses to settle.

But when it does, ah, then one can look about quietly and see what is there. One can lie in the waving valley grasses and admit that the valley is pleasant, too. Stillness and endings have a beauty of their own.

Like a jagged natural crystal, silently slicing from the rock.

Prologue to an Unwritten Memoir

I am an ungrateful child. I do know that.

It's true that I am grateful to have been let loose from Heaven, that glorious prison where there are no fleshly delights, no mangos, no tongue, no odor of jasmine or sex.

It's true that my mother worked hard, in all the ways that mothers do work, starting with splitting herself open to bring us in from the floating realms.

It's true that my father was our slave. All day he served a telephone and men with bigger destinies, and came home tired, defeated, and longing to be big himself.

And we were never badly hurt in any physical way – no broken bones, no cigarette burns. We never went hungry or slept without blankets. We got driven to soccer games and choir practice.

I can still hear my mother crying out from behind the bathroom door, *Can't you leave me alone even long enough to pee?*

I can imagine my father, though I wasn't there, shaking his head by my brother's deathbed, saying over and over, "My son… My son…"

But pain stays in the memory better than pleasure. At the name of a horror movie, one recalls the two-second scene of red and crème carnage, not the bluesy clouds of the opening credits. And though I have been thrown clear and cooling for decades on this pleasant plain, it is the bolting through the air in fragments of lava that I remember.

I am grateful for adulthood. I am grateful I lived through my childhood. I know they did the best they knew how to do.

I am glad I was let loose from heaven.

But I cannot yet be grateful for how it was done.

What Do You Write About, Anyway?

I write about human nature as I have observed it from my very small life and experience. Sometimes it seems like just confessional stuff: *I did this, here were my reasons.* But it is not about me, really. It is, *I did this. I am human. Aren't humans funny? What does this say about humans?* Sometimes I am asking, *You're human, too — what would you have done in this situation?* Sometimes I am asking, *Have you seen humans do this, too? What do you think about it?*

Humans fascinate me endlessly. There is really no predicting what they will do, no matter how well we may know any one of them. We all have so many layers, and only a few are known to those around us, even if we have lived with them for years. Layers in a personality may go all the way back to babyhood, and which of us is even fully aware of them? Even if you have had tons of therapy and think you know yourself well, one layer may react to another in ways previously unimagined.

Grief, for instance. Grief is very individual. When my brother died of AIDS, we all reacted differently. My mother responded with extreme mourning, falling into tears at the drop of a hat and discussing her son exhaustively, even with strangers. Under previous stresses, she had withdrawn and given everyone the silent treatment. My father was different — he reacted with anger, the male go-to. He was angry at Mom for crying all the time. He was angry with people at the funeral for hugging so much. He found it suspicious, being homophobic. My brother's homosexuality, coming from such a traditional family, added a twist that nobody could have predicted, changing the trajectory of their grief. I, on the other hand, who had no problem with that, froze in my grief and could not express it at all to these disapproving people, and became depressed and blurry. It took three years and a therapy group to come to terms with the feelings I could not express to my family, who did not accept him as he was.

And there I go again, using the personal to illustrate the universal. It's what I do. It's what I care about. I listen in coffee shops to other people's conversations. I watch the crowd at a wedding rather than dancing. And I write: *See? This is what I saw. This is what people do. What do you think of that? What does it mean?*

Corn Sweat

Cornsweat. The farm sits in the middle of an empty field, and all the surrounding fields are corn. The heat beats down, heat like angry words, punishing, merciless. Heat like a man with a sword, hanging over your neck. Sticky sweat from a man who is running. Your husband runs. You pick up his pants after his jog and they are soggy, rolled on themselves, twisted. You wonder how he can do it. You drop the underwear in the laundry basket, and go back to your iced tea.

Cornsweat. The woman in the farm house is pegging out the laundry. The sun beats on her head like a swear word. She lifts the sheet up to the line, and for a moment her vision goes white. What makes her live here, what is the attraction of a primitive farm house in rural America, with the nearest hospital 50 or 100 miles away? Or has the man's appeal faded, is it the kids, whose booties she hangs to dry? Is it the heavy silence, mile after mile of it, with nary a computer or iPod to break it? Does she watch TV? Or does she get her satisfaction from the rituals of cleaning, her creativity from cooking?

Cornsweat. There is no money here. America doesn't like to pay much for its produce. If it weren't for government subsidies, they would be done for. Last time somebody stayed in the hospital, they actually entertained the idea of burning down the barn for insurance. Just for a minute. Then they shook their heads and went back out to feed the hens.

Cornsweat when he sits on the harvester and the back of his hat grows greasy. Cornsweat callusing his fingers and the heels of his hands. Cornsweat when they tangle together at night, seeking relief among muggy sheets.

There's another baby. It makes horrible smells and cries in the heat. She puts aside her scrubbing, gets up off her knees, applies a clean washcloth to the creases of his dirty little bottom. Wipes the cornsweat away.

There has always been cornsweat. There always will be. It will never be winter again. It will never rain.

About the Author

Deborah Fruchey was born in California over 60 years ago. She tried to write her first book at the age of 8. Her first completed novel, *The Unwilling Heiress*, was chosen as a Best Book by the American Bookseller's Association in 1987. She has attended several colleges just for fun, never earning a degree, and has worked at everything from international banking to selling light bulbs over the phone. Her titles include flash fiction, poetry, comedy romances, and a self help manual. Deborah has appeared in a number of anthologies and is editor and publisher of the micro-press Last Laugh Productions.

In 2005 Deborah married musician Robert Hamaker (with whom she makes meditation albums), and became a full time author. She no longer knows why she bothered with anything else. She loves producing beautiful books for worthy authors.

In addition, she speaks for the National Alliance of Mental Illness in their "In Our Own Voice" program, as a result of her own experience with Bipolar Disorder. She coordinates this program for her local NAMI branch.

Connect with Deborah

www.lafruche.net

www.lastlaughproductions.org

www.strictly-east.org

Facebook: http://facebook.com/fruchey1

X: http://twitter.com/lafruche

Below please find a short excerpt from Deborah's previous flash fiction collection, **Priestess of Secrets***:*

The Minute We Die

"When they die we change our minds about them."
 — *Jennifer Michael Hecht*

The minute we die we become more valuable. We are suddenly a limited edition. Our failings aren't annoying any longer, since no one need endure them. They are instantly unimportant, though up until now they weighed equally in the balance with our good deeds. Suddenly, gossip about us is no longer interesting or delicious, it is petty and mean.

Once nothing can be changed, there is no excuse to criticize. We can never change people by complaining about them anyway. But people forget that about the living. Once we die, bygones are bygones. People who could not forgive us in life shrug and say, "It's all water under the bridge" (as if that had not been so before). And our good deeds are now almost haloed, as if they were the only acts that counted.

Why this insistence on not speaking ill of the dead? Is it just the impulse to accentuate pleasant memories? Or does it have darker roots, a primeval fear of spirits, the belief that the dead are not truly gone but can hear you and evince their displeasure? After all, how could one fight the vengeance of a ghost? You can't shoot them, run them out of town, or issue restraining orders. Hell, you can't get anyone to admit they exist. Yet they, if they chose, might do anything to you…things you could not imagine, could not undo. Is it fear of the deep dark that makes us write eulogies even for those we resent?

Think of *Dias de los Muertos*. Think of Chinese Ancestor worship. Think of expensive granite gravestones and memorial masses that go on for decades after the final breath. Do we truly believe the dead are gone? Or are they peeking over our shoulders, whispering to us, reminding us of what we should have done, should have said, murmuring without hope of the ways we could have helped them? Is it the dead we fear or our own consciences? Startling awake too late to all the glorious possible moments of kindness and understanding we missed because we were busy getting our morning coffee, making a buck, winning the argument, having our egos soothed. We would have to be kind tomorrow. We would resolve to pay attention later, when it was easier, when it cost less.

Then all at once it is too late to pay those debts, and we know we owe them. So we placate the fearsome dead, raise monuments to them, speak their praise. They are beyond hurt or insult or speeches or compliments, but once they have left their bones, they are no longer localized. They are everywhere, inescapable.

The dead are a fearful burden behind our eyes. We speak them fair so they will relax, close their eyes on us, go to sleep. "Rest in peace" is not a blessing, but a desperate incantation. We hold ceremonies and processions, we weep and pray. Go, for the love of God, lie down and leave us alone with our sins.

Abandoned

The car smelt like mold. It was out by the riverbank in the back pastures. Cassie went there when she wanted to think. Once, that jalopy had been a creature of time and motion. You entered it to move from one part of your life to another that you thought would be better. You entered it to transit.

Now it sat empty at the center of nothing, and it gave her a ringside seat on her personal journey. When she sat down in the cobwebby old cab and rustled a place for herself among the dried leaves on the bulging vinyl, she was stopping at a point that was neither A nor B. Life was in motion around her, and only she was still, watching the eddies of her own experience hit dry land and leave mute patterns on the shifting pebbles of beaches she hadn't reached yet.

An abandoned car is a place where somebody quit. They could have bought parts, done a diagnostic, pulled it into the shop for repairs; started back on the long road to rehabilitation. Or they could have sold the old model, turned it in for scrap, traded it for parts, towed it off and got something new. Those are the choices, aren't they? Go forward or go back. That's what they told you. But whoever left the car had not done either: they had just stopped, just driven it into the field and left it there, proof that there is a third option no one talks about. The option to quit: walk away, let time and weather and circumstantial factors finish the story, finish the car. It had never been registered to a new owner, but now it belonged to nobody. And in that way, it belonged to everybody.

So the car was sitting there quietly doing nothing, and sometimes Cassie joined it. She thought about the third option. They said she had to work things out with Earl, make her family survive. They said she had responsibilities. They said, you're a mother, there's no backing out of that. Life goes on, they said. If you divorce him, you'll just have to make a life for yourself and a disabled child; get a job and a babysitter and some new place to live. It'll be hard. Why not just put up with a little rough-housing on the odd Saturday night, a few bruises now and then, and just stop grumbling? Everybody knows what Earl's like. It's not like they blame you. And how could you date and find somebody new with that sick boy wagging at your heels all the time? You can't have your youth back. You can't unmake your choices.

But Cassie looked at the car and thought of leaving her family behind like that. Don't fix it; don't replace it; don't provide for it – just walk off and leave it in a field somewhere. Let their memories of her grow sunburned and moldy and collect dried leaves. Let the glove compartment hang open with its cheap trash collapsing outward. People would talk about her. But they did anyway. She'd go to Topeka, be a single woman again, not young but youngish. A woman with no past, no ties. The child would still be registered to her, but she'd leave it in the fields to the kindness of nature; and in the end, it would belong to everybody.

Autumn Couple

Marisa had married at 46, and she wondered how many years they'd get. 40? 30? Would it be enough? How much of it would be under the tense gun of disablement, one partner looking after another, gulping resentment while the other shuffled, whale-slow, to the toilet? Would his eyes cease to contain him? Would she be single in all but name for a good 20 of those years?

So many things she left to him to do, in the way of Fifties women. He paid the bills, yes, fixed the computer and swept the gutters out. He carried the heavy stuff, dug trenches. When she had lived alone, she had done these things for herself – or not at all. It was beginning to annoy her, how many things he maintained in cherry condition which she would have allowed to dilapidate themselves naturally.

Did that make her slovenly, or him uptight?

Their rhythms, too, were different. She required rest and contemplation, and good reasons to do anything, or the mood to do it. He just acted – as if he had no preferences at all, like a duck or a squid that acts on prerecorded prompts. He would get home from work, see a fallen tree branch, and head straight for the garage for tools to cut it up. She, with her tea in hand, would have been looking at it and deciding whether she wanted to do this, for an hour. He got out of bed directly into the shower and thence to clothes. She got to the shower two hours after waking, debating over coffee whether the day deserved her dressing for it.

What would happen to the house when he slowed down and stopped? For surely a fuse would burst somewhere. Like a fountain running too long with too little water, the pump would burn dry. She thought with dismay of the house settling into genteel decrepitude, and the neighbors talking about her. Would she still care, if they were not looking? The grass would wave itself in the breeze, crowned by little seed-heads; when the bicycle tires popped, she would just stop riding.

What was it in her that accepted atrophy, the world spinning down to a stop with a glug and a whisper? What was it in her that could watch the cobwebs grow and continue drinking its tea, and when the hot water main broke, just drink it cold with perfect placid balance?

She would fit right into old age, she thought. He would not fit — he would break. She loved him. But she wondered if she'd like it, not having him show her up in her inherent entropy.

She knew she was not The American Way. Perhaps she was something more ancient. She suspected her way hurt less.

None of that stopped the guilt.

She adored him peevishly, like a favorite gorgeous parakeet that insists on chirruping all through your afternoon nap.

Other Books by Deborah Fruchey

Fiction

The Unwilling Heiress
(Walker Company, 1987)

A Scandalous Creature
(Last Laugh Productions, 2009)

Priestess of Secrets
(Last Laugh Productions, 2017)

Shattered Windows
(Last Laugh Productions, 2024)

Non-Fiction

Mental Illness Ain't for Sissies
Steps & Strategies that Work
(Last Laugh Productions, 2020)

Poetry

Armadillo:
Selected Works 1979 to 2009
(Cyborg Productions, 2011)

Three Kinds of Dark
(Zeitgeist Press, 2020)

Hint: poems
(Last Laugh Productions, 2024)

Edited by Deborah Fruchey:

Eye Masks
By Rudy Jon Tanner
(Last Laugh Productions, 2023)

For Whoever Thinks a Piano is Furniture
By Rudy Jon Tanner
(Last Laugh Productions, 2023)

Gypsy
By Steve Arntson
(Last Laugh Productions, 2022)

Touchstones
By Maria Elizabeth Rosales
(Last Laugh Productions, 2021)

Armageddon Bootcamp
by Maria Elizabeth Rosales
(Last Laugh Productions, 2021)

Hollow Quills & Jackal Fur
by Bana Witt
(Zeitgeist Press, 2020)

If Thirst Were Proof of Water
by Rudy Jon Tanner
(Zeitgeist Press, 2020)

Bat Flower:
Poems, Plays and Other Perversions
by Vampyre Mike Kassel
(Last Laugh Productions, 2019)

Our Lady of Telegraph Avenue:
Tributes to Julia Vinograd
(Zeitgeist Press, 2019)

Royal Pond
by Ven Olac
(CreateSpace, 2015)

Color Cards & Self-Healing
by Jean Luo
(CreateSpace, 2013)

Other Offerings from Last Laugh Productions

Eye Masks, by Rudy Jon Tanner

What Still Matters, by Johanna Ely

We'll Always Have Stockton, by Steve Arntson

The Worlds According to Loki, 2nd Edition, by Vampyre Mike Kassel

For Whoever Thinks a Piano is Furniture, by Rudy Jon Tanner

The Hall of Painted Sonnets, Sonnets by Steve Arntson, Art by Diane Lee Moomey

Embodied (hardcover), by Jan Dederick

*Gypsy & Other Poem*s, by Steve Arntson

Armageddon Bootcamp...and other poems (hardcover), by Maria Elizabeth Rosales

Three Kinds of Dark (ebook, hardcover), by Deborah L. Fruchey

Touchstones (hardcover), by Maria Elizabeth Rosales

Priestess of Secrets, by Deborah L. Fruchey

Bat Flower: poems, plays & other perversions, by Vampyre Mike Kassel

Armadillo: selected poems 1979 to 2009 (ebook, hardcover), by Deborah L. Fruchey

Color Cards & Self Healing, by Jean Luo

The Colors of Sound (companion CD or MP3), performed & composed by Robert Hamaker

A Scandalous Creature, by Deborah L. Fruchey

Mental Illness Ain't for Sissies, by Deborah L. Fruchey

The Unwilling Heiress (paperback, ebook), by Deborah L. Fruchey

Island Journey (Instrumental CD or MP3), composed & performed by Robert M. Hamaker

Island Journey (Narrated, Meditation CD or MP3), by Robert M. Hamaker, narrated by Deborah Fruchey

Crystal Connections (CD or MP3), by Robert M. Hamaker & Erik Satie *(Gymnopodie #1)*

Crystalline Sleep (Binaural Beats CD or MP3), by Robert M. Hamaker

Opus De Funk (single, MP3), composed by Horace Silver, performed by *Interplay*

www.lastlaughproductions.org
logo by Bradleigh Stockwell

www.ingramcontent.com/pod-product-compliance
Lightning Source LLC
Chambersburg PA
CBHW071236170626
46809CB00008BA/3083